Jack and the Hurricane

story by Joshua Goudie
art by Craig Goudie

Tuckamore Books
a Creative Publishers imprint

St. John's, Newfoundland and Labrador
2014

Canada Council for the Arts Conseil des Arts du Canada Canada Newfoundland Labrador

We gratefully acknowledge the financial support of the Canada Council for the Arts, the Government of Canada through the Canada Book Fund (CBF), and the Government of Newfoundland and Labrador through the Department of Tourism, Culture and Recreation for our publishing program.

Cover Design and Illustrations by Craig Goudie
Printed on acid-free paper

Published by
TUCKAMORE BOOKS
an imprint of CREATIVE BOOK PUBLISHING
a Transcontinental Inc. associated company
P.O. Box 8660, Stn. A
St. John's, Newfoundland and Labrador A1B 3T7

Printed in Canada by:
Marquis imprimeur inc.

Library and Archives Canada Cataloguing in Publication

Goudie, Joshua, 1985-, author
     Jack and the Hurricane / story by Joshua Goudie ; art by Craig Goudie.

ISBN 978-1-77103-059-5 (bound)

     I. Goudie, Craig, 1960-, illustrator II. Title.

PS8613.O824J34 2014   jC813'.6   C2014-904694-4

To my grandparents
Vivian and Chesley Verge and Ruth and Carl Goudie

... and to your grandparents, too!
J.G.

Jack's grandmother had been standing at the window for hours. The rain had been falling for even longer. "Oh dear," she said, as she watched the trees bend against the wind. "It doesn't look like anyone will be getting outside today."

"Why not?" asked Jack.

"Because," she replied, "that out there is a hurricane."

Jack had never heard of a hurricane.

"Looks like these cupcakes won't be making it to your cousin's house after all. And on her birthday, too. Oh dear!"

Jack had been looking forward to his cousin Erin's birthday party all week. He was sad that she wouldn't have his grandmother's cupcakes for her party. And with everybody stuck at home, he was even sadder that there might not be any guests at her party, either.

"Oh dear," said Jack's grandmother. "Now the power's gone, too. It certainly is getting bad out there. I'll have to go downstairs to get some candles and flashlights so we won't be sitting in the dark. Oh dear!"

Now there wouldn't be any lights at the party, thought Jack. This thought made him saddest of all.

That's when Jack got an idea. He knew what his grandmother would say if he told her his plan, so before she came back upstairs, he slipped on his rain pants, zipped up his raincoat and jumped into his rain boots. Then he grabbed the plate of cupcakes off the table and ran out the door.

"There may not be lights and there may not be guests," he said to himself, "but this party will have cupcakes."

Jack held on to his hat with one hand and the plate of cupcakes with the other. As he walked, the water on the road splished and sloshed up over his boots, soaking him all the way through to his socks.

"Grandma was right," said Jack. "It is bad out here." For a moment he thought about turning back... but only for a moment.

That's when Jack saw his neighbour, Mr. Sweetapple. He was standing in his basement doorway tossing bucket after bucket of water out into the yard. The hurricane had brought down so much rain that Mr. Sweetapple's basement had flooded.

But Jack didn't know this. He imagined that Mr. Sweetapple must have overflowed his bathtub, turning his house into a giant water slide and now he was having to clean up his mess.

"What are you doing out here?" asked Mr. Sweetapple when he saw Jack. "Don't you know this is a hurricane?"

"Of course I know," said Jack, "but I've got to get these cupcakes to my cousin's birthday party."

"You really shouldn't be out here," said Mr. Sweetapple. "Why don't you turn around and head home?"

"I already thought about that," said Jack, "but I've got to deliver these cupcakes."

"If you say so," said Mr. Sweetapple. "Say, all this work has given me quite an appetite. Do you think maybe I could have one of those?"

Jack looked down at the plate in his hands. He did have a whole plate full.

"Good luck," said Mr. Sweetapple as Jack started off again. "And thanks for the cupcake."

"Good luck with the water slide," replied Jack.

The rain continued to come down harder and harder. Now as Jack walked, the water on the road was splashing and sploshing up over his rain pants, soaking him all the way through to his overalls.

"Maybe Grandma and Mr. Sweetapple were right," said Jack, as he held on to his plate. "It is bad out here." For a moment he thought about turning back... but only for a moment.

Off in the distance, Jack saw a fire truck. The firefighters were using their trucks to block a road that had washed away.

But Jack didn't know this. Jack imagined that the wind must have blown all the town's cats up into a tree and now the firefighters were there to get them down.

"What are you doing outside?" asked one of the firefighters when he saw Jack. "Don't you know this is a hurricane?"

"Of course I know," said Jack, "but I've got to get these cupcakes to my cousin's birthday party."

"You really shouldn't be out here," said the firefighter. "Why don't you turn around and head home?"

"I already thought about that," said Jack, "but I've got to deliver these cupcakes."

"If you say so," said the firefighter. "By the way, we've been out here an awful long time. Do you think maybe we could have some of those?"

Jack looked down at the plate in his hands. He did still have almost a plate full.

The firefighters waved as Jack started on his journey again. "Thanks," they said, "and be careful."

"Good luck with the cats," replied Jack.

The rain continued to come down harder and harder. Now as Jack walked, the water on the road was squishing and squashing up over his raincoat soaking him all the way through to his underwear.

"Maybe Grandma, Mr. Sweetapple and the firefighters were right," said Jack, as he held on tight to his plate. "It is bad out here." For a moment he thought about turning back... but only for a moment.

Jack was walking with his head down when a great voice boomed above him. "What are you doing out here?" it said. "Don't you know this is a hurricane?"

Jack looked up and saw a group of soldiers standing around him. They had been going door to door making sure everyone was safe in their homes.

But Jack didn't know this. When Jack saw them he imagined they might be getting ready to fight the hurricane.

"Of course I know," said Jack, "but I've got to make sure these cupcakes get to my cousin's birthday party."

"You really shouldn't be out here," said the general. "Why don't you turn around and march back home?"

"I already thought about that," said Jack, "but I've got to deliver these cupcakes."

"Well," said the general, "if you're on a mission we won't stop you. But before you go, we've been working pretty hard for some time without anything to eat. Do you think maybe we could have a few of those cupcakes?"

Jack looked down at the plate in his hands. There were still a few cupcakes left.

"Thank-you," called the general, "and stay safe."

"Good luck fighting those clouds," replied Jack.

Jack hadn't thought that rain could do so much damage. All around him he could see trees lying on their sides and giant cracks forming in the roads. "Maybe Grandma, Mr. Sweetapple, the firefighters and the general were right," said Jack. "It is bad out here." For a moment he thought about turning back... but only for a moment.

When Jack finally reached his cousin Erin's house, he was a mess.

"Jack!" shouted Erin. "What are you doing here? Don't you know this is a hurricane?"

"Of course I know," said Jack. "That's why I had to make sure these cupcakes got to your party."

"But Jack," said Erin, "because of the hurricane, my party will have to wait until next week."

"Oh," said Jack.

Just then, Jack and Erin heard a rumble. They ran to the window to see a huge military truck roll right up to the front door. Then, out from the truck popped the general, the firefighter, Mr. Sweetapple and, finally, Jack's grandmother.

"Jack!" said his grandmother once they were all inside. "Thank goodness I finally found you. I had to talk to Mr. Sweetapple who sent me to the firefighters who sent me to the army just to find you."

"All in a day's work, ma'am," said the general.

"Well," said Erin, "with everyone here, why not have a birthday party now?"

"Hooray!" shouted everyone but Jack.

"Sorry," said Jack, "but I don't know what kind of party it will be with only one cupcake."

"Well it's a good thing I made more cupcakes," said Jack's grandmother, as she brought out another plate from her backpack. "But Jack, don't you ever do anything so foolish as going out into a hurricane again."

"I won't," said Jack.

"Promise?" said everyone.

"I promise," said Jack.

"Good," said Jack's grandmother, shaking her head. "What am I ever going to do with you?"

"...Oh dear!"

In an emergency help can come in many different shapes and sizes. Sometimes, it can even come in ways you wouldn't expect.

In September of 2010, Hurricane Igor swept across the province of Newfoundland and Labrador, bringing with it lots of wind and rain. Things became so bad that a lot of people lost their electricity and many bridges and roads were washed away. In some cases entire houses were lifted right out of the ground.

What is so remarkable about this is not just how severe the damage was, but how everyone in the province and country came together to help out. When someone's house flooded, neighbours were there to take them in and offer assistance. When heat or power was lost, the fire department set up safe places for people to go get warm. And when people were getting hungry, the military made sure there was plenty of food and water available.

Events like this are rare here on the island but it's important to remember that when there is an emergency, always listen to an adult you trust, like a parent or teacher. They can make sure that you stay safe!

Joshua Goudie was born in Grand Falls-Windsor and now lives and writes in St. John's. His work has been published in *The Telegram* as well as in several Cuffer anthologies. In 2013, he was short-listed for the Newfoundland and Labrador Credit Union's Fresh Fish Award.

...Josh is Craig's son.

Craig Goudie has been working as a visual artist for over thirty years, producing work for galleries, serving on local and provincial arts-related boards and teaching high school art. His artwork hangs in government, corporate and private collections.

...Craig is Josh's dad.